**Fountaindale
Public Library District**

300 W. Briarcliff Road
Bolingbrook, Illinois
60439

Nattie Witch

by Ruth Rosner

Harper & Row, Publishers

FOR MARIAN PARRY

Nattie Witch
Copyright © 1989 by Ruth Rosner
Printed in the U.S.A. All rights reserved.
1 2 3 4 5 6 7 8 9 10
First Edition

Library of Congress Cataloging-in-Publication Data
Rosner, Ruth.
  Nattie witch.
  Summary: Nattie the witch girl seems to have a normal
day—eating breakfast, going to school, and playing with
her pet—except that her breakfast is newt
loops, her school is a witch school, and her pet is a
lizard.
  [1. Witches—Fiction]
PZ7.R71955Nat 1989   [E]   89-2135
ISBN 0-06-025098-4
ISBN 0-06-025099-2 (lib. bdg.)

Every morning, Nattie's mother
gets her up for school.

Nattie goes back to bed
for just one more minute.

Then she takes a bath . . .

fixes her hair . . .

gets dressed . . .

and makes breakfast.

If she's late for school,

her father gives her a ride.

Nattie kisses him good-bye and

runs down the hall to her classroom.

She's glad to start the day's work

and see her friends Charlie and Roxanne.

Nattie loves science.

She also loves art . . .

and gym.

Sometimes she talks too much
to her neighbors.

"Pay attention, Natalya," says her teacher,
"or I'll have to move your desk."

At noon, Nattie goes down
to the cafeteria.

Then she plays "bat the ball" at recess.
She can send a ball high over the fence.

When recess is over, she takes dancing

and violin.

Her last class is swimming. "I can turn the
worst swimmers into little fish," promises the coach.

After school, Nattie goes home with Charlie
and Roxanne. They take long walks with their pets.

Their favorite game is hide-and-seek.

In the late afternoon,
Nattie likes the quiet of her room.

She dreams of what she'll be
when she grows up.

poof!

Her mother calls at five-thirty. She must watch
her baby brother while her parents get dinner.

At the table, they all talk about their day.

poof!

Then they tell stories by the fire. No one can make

a story come to life like Nattie's father.

Bedtime always comes too soon for Nattie.

Her parents hug and kiss her, and say:
"Good night, Nattie. Sleep tight.
Don't let the bedbugs bite."
Nattie falls fast asleep.